The Wit & Wisdom
of Freddy and
His Friends

The Wit & Wisdom of Freddy

and His Friends

Illustrations by Kurt Wiese • Introduction by Michael Cart
Sarah Koslosky, Contributing Editor

THE OVERLOOK PRESS
Woodstock & New York

ACKNOWLEDGMENTS

The Wit & Wisdom of Freddy and His Friends has been a collaborative undertaking made possible by a dedicated group of Freddy enthusiasts. Special thanks go to eleven-year-old Sarah Koslosky, a home schooler who read through the books in the series and gathered additional selections from her fellow members of the Friends of Freddy. Sarah was a wellspring of ideas and a careful consultant whose contributions helped bring the book forward. Sarah's father, Pierce, ever affable and dependable, was a champion of the project from the start. The publishers would also like to acknowledge Michael Cart, Albert DePetrillo, Kelly W. Rush, Jessie Chaffee, Mannar Wong, and Lee Secrest, whose contributions helped *Wit & Wisdom* capture the spirit of Freddy.

Pierce Koslosky, Jr., acknowledges the efforts of Hannah Koslosky, Candice Koslosky, Tom Collins, Lynn Bartholomew, Kevin Parker, Alice Tracy, Paul Annis, Jill Morgan, Wendy E. Betts, Ivan Lanningham, James A. Inglehart, Laird Blackwell, Michael B. Pinkey, Dusty Gres, and all the Friends of Freddy who helped with the the project.

Remembering the Freddy Books and Their Creator, Walter R. Brooks

by Michael Cart

Freddy the Pig was born one hot, lonely summer in the early 1920s when an advertising man named Walter R. Brooks sat down and, out of sheer boredom, wrote a book. The whimsical story that resulted—about a group of animals who, one winter, decide to migrate from their Upstate New York farm to Florida in search of warmer weather—was published in 1927 with the title *To and Again*. And, as history has proven, not only a pig but also one of the most popular children's book series in publishing history was born. Ultimately there would be twenty-six books recounting the adventures of Freddy and his other talking animal friends. Though the superior pig was only a member of the supporting cast in Brooks's first book, he proved so witty and wise that he quickly commanded center stage in later titles. Walter modestly professed surprise at this: "Pigs in general are not built for the heroic role," he wrote. "I am rather puzzled myself to know why Freddy, rather than a dog or cat, should have become my permanent hero. Maybe because Kurt Wiese, who illustrates the stories, draws such very sympathetic pigs."

Freddy became a permanent hero because he was Walter's alter ego—or was it the other way around? Consider their many similarities: for starters, both were poets. In fact, Walter's very first published work was a sonnet titled "Haunted" that appeared in *The Century* magazine in 1915; Freddy's first poem, "Spring" (modestly signed "Shakespeare, Jr."), was published in the Centerboro *Guardian*. Both also played an unlikely combination: guitar and football. As a schoolboy in 1902, Walter played left end for the second team at the Mohegan Lake Military Academy, while Freddy played tackle for Centerboro High School. Both were artists, too. Freddy cut a particularly dashing figure in smock and beret (see *Freddy and Mr. Camphor*, 1944); Walter wasn't as dashing but he was the more serious artist, having actually studied painting at New York's School of Related Arts. And both were book lovers, of course. Walter once recalled that, as a boy, he had read "a good deal more than anybody but my mother had thought was good for me," and when he grew up, his hobby became learning foreign languages (he could read six or seven). In his later years he was even a part-time bookseller, a bit like Mr. Tweedle in *Freddy the Pilot* (1952).

Both Freddy and Walter were newspaper editors; the former, of course, was at the helm of *The Bean Home News,* while Walter was one of four assistant editors of his school newspaper, *The Moheganite*. When he grew up, he also worked as a magazine editor and even served on the editorial staff of the famous *New Yorker* magazine in 1932–33.

Freddy was a politician, and Walter never met—or imagined—a politician he didn't love to lampoon. Both had banking in their blood: Freddy was founder and President of the First Animal Bank, while Walter's grandfather and uncle were bank presidents in Rome, New York. Both pig and man disliked winter, and neither was fond of work. Walter once cheerfully acknowledged that "the four things I really dislike are sweetbreads, spiritualistic seances, cold weather, and work."

What else did they have in common? Well, Freddy was a detective and Walter loved reading about detectives. In fact, as book review editor of a magazine called *The Outlook and Independent* in 1929, he was the first important reviewer to discover the work of the now legendary mystery novelist Dashiell Hammett. Which brings us to one last resemblance of note: Walter, a smallish man who stood barely 5'6" tall, looked, with his fair complexion and round face, "like Freddy in one of his disguises," author Henry S. F. Cooper told me some years ago, and he should know, for, as a boy, he once had the good fortune to have lunch with Walter.

Alter egos? You bet! And you know what else? I suspect they were best friends, too.

Freddy's friend and faithful Boswell, Walter R. Brooks (the "R." stands for "Rollin"), was born on January 9, 1886, in Rome, New York, which, in those days, must have looked a lot like the village of Centerboro, where much of the action of the Freddy books takes place. His mother, Fannie, was the daughter of Samuel Barron Stevens, not only a prominent banker but also among Rome's first mayors. His father, William Walter Brooks, was a University of Leipzig–educated music teacher and the son of Dr. Walter Rollin Brooks, Walter's namesake and a prominent Baptist theologian who was on the faculty of Madison University, which today is called Colgate University.

Walter's family expected him to become a doctor, but he dropped out of medical school in 1909 and became a writer, instead. At first he wrote advertising and publicity for the American Red Cross, but in 1915 he published "Harden's Chance," a short story for adults; it was the first of the more than two hundred that would follow over the next forty years. Of Walter's many short stories, which were published in *The Saturday Evening Post* and other leading magazines of the day, the most celebrated are the twenty-five he wrote about a talking horse named "Ed." For, yes, Walter R. Brooks was, indeed, the creator not only of Freddy but also of the famous Mr. Ed.

He also published two novels for adults. The first, *The Romantic Liars,* was serialized in *Country Gentleman* magazine in 1925. The second, *Ernestine Takes Over,* was published by Morrow in 1935.

Of all of Walter's works, though, it is the Freddy books that are the most beloved and, frankly, the most enduring. They are classics of children's literature and are among the first authentically funny books published for young readers in America. Because Walter respected his readers and never, ever wrote down to them, his books have always been enjoyed by both children and adults.

At the outset, the Freddy books appeared only sporadically, but starting in 1939, Walter wrote one per year, and children all across America—including me—waited breathlessly for the month of October and the appearance of the new "Freddy."

The countless readers who grew up with the books will remember that *To and Again,* the first, was followed by *More To and Again* (1930), in which the Bean Farm animals take another trip, not south this time but north, all the way to the North Pole where they meet Santa Claus. (*To and Again* and *More To and Again* were later retitled *Freddy Goes to Florida* and *Freddy Goes to the North Pole*.) In 1932, *Freddy the Detective,* the book that most critics call the best in the series, appeared. It was followed in 1936 by *The Story of Freginald,* a tale about a talented bear who joins a circus. Though Freddy is only a minor character in this one, it is important to the series because it introduced Boomschmidt's Colossal and Unparalleled Circus, and it is the first in which the animals talk to human beings. In previous titles they had only talked to other animals. Other early titles include *The Clockwork Twin* (1937), in which—for the first time—Freddy disguises himself as an old woman, and *Wiggins for President* (1939; later retitled *Freddy the Politician*), in which Freddy founds both the First Animal Republic and the First Animal Bank (who says pigs are lazy!). In *Freddy's Cousin Weedly* the animals put on a play that Freddy has written, an activity that was surely inspired by Walter's own childhood when, as he recalled, "we wrote and put on plays up in our barn. The first writing I did was part of an act in one of those plays."

Every Freddy fan has his or her favorite title. Many readers are fond of the one that followed Weedly: *Freddy and the Ignormus* (1941). Its popularity is due, I suspect, to the fact that it is the first Freddy title that might be called a ghost story and, as such, includes not only laughs but also shudders. A later title, *Freddy Goes Camping* (1948), is even more clearly a ghost story and reflects both Walter's love for that genre and for camping, too, for he was an inveterate outdoorsman and an amateur naturalist, talents that Freddy would display in *Freddy and the Popinjay* (1945).

Freddy was a pig of many parts, and throughout the 1940s he appeared as an intrepid balloonist, a pied piper, a magician, and, in the 1950s, a cowboy, a pilot, and a traveler into outer space in *Freddy and the Space Ship* (1953), the book that, in my estimation, is the funniest in the entire series—high praise, indeed. Nothing lasts forever, alas, and in October 1958 the last Freddy book, *Freddy and the Dragon,* was published. It appeared posthumously, for Walter R. Brooks had died on August 17 of that year.

Freddy's fans are a diverse lot, but every one of them whom I have ever met has one thing in common: a vivid and recurring dream in which a new, never-before-seen Freddy book is found. I have had the dream many times myself and know, only too well, the heartache of waking to discover it was only a dream.

But wait! That dream has at last become a reality in the book you hold in your hands. *The Wit & Wisdom of Freddy and His Friends* is the first all-new Freddy book in forty-one years.

Savor it, for the delicious quotations you will discover here capture the humor—and the heart—of this wonderful series and remind us, as well, of how very American these books are in their celebration of such virtues as honesty, bravery, responsibility, and, yes, common sense.

But don't think this talk of "virtues" means that this is a didactic or moralistic collection. It is, instead, a celebration of imagination, of the joy of language, and of humor. The sound of laughter is never stilled in these happy pages, and the joy of friendship suffuses the entire enterprise.

But enough from me. Freddy and his friends are waiting for you in the pages that follow. I know you will enjoy their company as much as I do.

Friendship

Miss Peebles was quite old, and some people would have thought she was funny looking.... But Freddy did not think she looked funny any more than most of the people in Centerboro did. Because if you like people a lot, it doesn't matter what they look like.

—Freddy and the Popinjay

"Any friend of the sheriff's a friend

of mine, whether he be man, beast

or insect; whether he talks, sings or

merely grunts."

—Mr. Golcher, **Freddy and the Perilous Adventure**

"Why do it at all?" said Jinx. "Why
should we have to put up with his
nonsense just because you think
that way down inside him there's
some good qualities?"

"It's like digging for buried treasure,"
said Freddy.

—Freddy and the Popinjay

"I like my friends to look like
friends, not like something I dream
about when I've eaten too many
angleworms."

—Samuel the Mole, **Freddy and the Flying Saucer Plans**

When [their friend] was quarrel-some they didn't laugh and they didn't argue—they went away and let him alone. And in a little while he'd come around and apologize for having been so cantankerous.

—The Story of Freginald

His eyes prickled a little, and then he shook his head angrily. "This is the kind of summer I wanted," he said, "and I'm going to enjoy it if it kills me!" Then he laughed. "I do enjoy it, of course," he said. "Only it makes me realize how fond I am of my friends when I see them after being away for a while."

—**Freddy and Mr. Camphor**

"To desert your friends when they're in want and danger—I never heard such cowardly nonsense!"

—Henrietta the Hen,
Freddy Goes To the North Pole

"Are we going to see Mr. Boomschmidt,

our benefactor, put upon and

insulted in our own tent and not

raise hoof nor claw to avenge it?"

—Leo the Lion, **The Story of Freginald**

"These sailors are nice and friendly
to me, but they're big fat men, all
pork-eaters—I can tell a pork-eater
just by the way he looks at me, so
greedy it makes me fairly blush
sometimes—and what's friendship
to a hungry man?"

—Freddy, **Freddy Goes To the North Pole**

Rats are not loyal and do not understand loyalty. That Freddy should stay loyal to Mr. Bean, when it was to his advantage to go over to the other side, was something that Simon found it difficult to believe. And so he was not hard to convince that Freddy would betray old friends for a more comfortable position.

—Freddy and Simon the Dictator

"That's the trouble with having a lot of money—nobody ever comes just to see me. They always want to sell me something, or get me to give money to something, or—or something. Always something to do with money, at any rate. Never just friendly talk about the weather, and politics, and—and food."

—Mr. Camphor, **Freddy and Mr. Camphor**

Since I made friends with you and your family and promised to leave you alone, I haven't seen hide nor hair, nor tooth nor tail of anything I could hunt. Friendship's all very well, but it spoils lots of good sport."

—Jinx the Cat, **Freddy Goes To the North Pole**

"Flowers and friendship, eh? Flowers I ain't got much use for. Hundreds here, and only one button hole to put 'em in. But friendship—yes; friendship I go for."

—Mr. Doty, **Freddy Plays Football**

"I've missed you animals; began to think all my old friends had deserted me."

"There's no friend like an old friend," put in Bannister.

Freddy grinned, remembering how Mr. Camphor and Bannister were always arguing about proverbs, and testing them out to see whether they were really true or not.

—**Freddy Goes Camping**

Freddy was his friend, and a friend was worth many times five thousand dollars.

—Freddy and Simon the Dictator

"As a lifelong friend and companion of animals, I count as my most cherished friends members of the porcine race. And a pig—*as* pig—can be a very handsome animal. I should be the last to deny it."

—Mr. Boomschmidt,
Freddy and the Perilous Adventure

[Robert the dog] began with some discussion of the traditional friendship between dog and man. The dog, he said, was man's elder brother. He guarded and watched over him; no other animal so had man's trust and liking. Their relationship was founded on mutual affection.

—Freddy and Simon the Dictator

"Nay, look not so downcast, lad....
Hast ever known a Wilson to flinch
from the fight? We'll stand by thee
to the last skunk."

As Sniffy had intended it made
Freddy grin.

"Oh, sure," he said, "And I'll fight to
the last pig. Only I *am* the last pig."

—Freddy the Pilot

After Mr. Golcher had gone, Freddy went back to the cow barn. He was pretty pleased to find that Mr. Bean really believed in him, even though

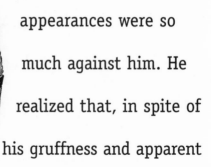

appearances were so much against him. He realized that, in spite of his gruffness and apparent indifference, the farmer was a real friend—much more of a friend than some of the animals who were always protesting their friendship.

—Freddy and the Perilous Adventure

The bell clanged and bonged and made so much noise that he [Freddy] couldn't hear whether his friends were coming to his rescue or not; but he didn't need to hear them—he knew they'd come.

—**Freddy the Magician**

"It's easy enough to do things for a
friend in the daytime, but when
you sit up after bedtime to do
them, that's something different!"

—Freddy, **Freddy and the Bean Home News**

"I guess there's something about everybody on this farm you and I don't like. Even our best friends. But if they're friends, you just have to shut your eyes to such things. Usually they aren't very important."

—Mrs. Wiggins, **Freddy Plays Football**

"I know that when

you're in trouble it is good to see

a friend's face—even if it's only

a cow's."

—Mrs. Wiggins, **Freddy and the Bean Home News**

Bravery

"We can appreciate courage, my

friends, and we can honor it,

even in an enemy."

—Jinx the Cat, **Freddy and Simon the Dictator**

People who are scared are hardly ever very clear about what scared them. Freddy told Number Twenty-One that. "If you'd seen what it was that scared you," he said, "you probably wouldn't be scared any more. Because the more you know about a thing, the less scary it is. And if you know all about it, you find it isn't anything to be scared of at all."

—**Freddy and the Ignormus**

"Anyway, Theodore, we have
explored the Big Woods."

"And got g-good and scared," said
the frog. "I guess I was wrong to
say that you couldn't be brave and
cowardly at the same tut-tut, I
mean time. Because we were brave
too, to go in at all."

"I guess," said Freddy, "that all
brave deeds are like that. Only
later, when the people who did
them tell about them, they forget
the cowardly part. Maybe it would
be just as well if we did the same
thing. After all, we *did* go in."

—Freddy and the Ignormus

The six adventurers, who, like all the brave spirits who have made history and sailed unknown seas and charted unknown continents in the past, cared less for ease than for glory and laughed at danger and hardship.

—Freddy Goes To the North Pole

"The Big Woods are perfectly safe,"
he muttered. "I *know* they're safe.
Nothing to be scared of. Nothing."
And then he took a little card out
of his pocket, on which, before he
left home, he had typed the words:
"There isn't any Ignormus."
"There," he said to himself, "you
see? There it is in black and white.
There isn't any such animal." For
Freddy, like lots of other people,
believed things more easily when
he saw them in print than he did
when he just heard them.

—Freddy and the Ignormus

I suppose this was the bravest speech Freddy had ever made, and in the course of his adventures he had made quite a number. But though the speech was brave, he didn't feel very brave inside. His tail in fact had come completely uncurled, as it always did when he was scared. For though Freddy was brave, he was not fearless; indeed most apparently fearless acts are done by people who are just shivering inside. That's what bravery usually is.

—**Freddy and the Spaceship**

Freddy was determined. He was
really quite a courageous pig. I
don't mean that he wasn't scared;
he was so scared thinking about it
sometimes that his teeth chattered

and his tail came
completely uncurled.
But he didn't propose
to let being scared
interfere with what
he intended to do.

—**Freddy the Cowboy**

Freddy . . . wasn't any coward, either. One time, several years ago, he had led a charge right up to the muzzle of the shot-gun that was pointed at him. . . . Of course he had known that the gun wasn't loaded, but still it was a brave thing to do. But to charge on a boy with a slingshot wasn't brave, it was just foolhardy.

—Freddy and the Popinjay

"I suppose after you've jumped out and scared everybody you know a dozen times, it kind of loses its point. You want to go on to bigger and better things."

—Jinx the Cat, **Freddy and Simon the Dictator**

"Lots of folks wouldn't mind dying a hero's death in a good cause—but to perish looking like a silly fool ain't got anything grand about it."

—Hank the Horse, **Freddy and the Popinjay**

Freddy didn't like dark woods much either. It wasn't that he was a coward. Faced with a real danger, he could be as brave as anyone. Or almost. But he had a vivid imagination, and to such people imaginary dangers are much more awful than real ones.

—Freddy and the Men from Mars

He discovered suddenly that he was enjoying himself. He had only been scared because he had thought he ought to be scared, but after all he was having one of the most remarkable experiences of his long and colorful career.

—**Freddy and the Perilous Adventure**

"Now, now, animals," said Mrs. Bean

calmly. "There's nothing to be

ashamed of in being scared. You're

wrong, Quik, to blame Freddy for it.

But you're wrong, too, Freddy to

pretend you weren't."

—Freddy the Cowboy

"I used to like to run round at

night; all mice do. But now when-

ever I'm up after twelve, I hear

footsteps coming after me and at

every corner see giant cats with

phosphorescent eyes."

—Freddy Goes To the North Pole

"That's the funny thing about adventures. I've had my share of them in my time, as you know, and my experience is that either you're too busy to think whether you're enjoying them or not, or else you're just scared. And yet there must be something about them that you like, too, or else you wouldn't go on trying to have more."

—Freddy, **Freddy and the Perilous Adventure**

Freddy couldn't help putting on a bold and fearless expression when he said this; he didn't really want to show off in front of [Rabbit No.] 23, but the admiration in the rabbit's eyes was too much for him. After all, if you see that someone thinks you are a hero, you at least have to try to look like one.

—Freddy Rides Again

"He's trying to scare Condiment into marrying Lorna, just as Condiment is trying to scare Rose into marrying him. I mean, the one that loses will be the one that gets the scaredest."

—Mr. Boomschmidt, **Freddy the Pilot**

"That's the trouble with a reputation

for bravery: you have to live up

to it."

—Freddy, **Freddy and the Perilous Adventure**

"I just pretended to be scared. . . .

That's what you should have

done. . . . Trouble with you is you

don't know how to play. If some-

body put a jack-lantern on your

porch Hallowe'en night, you'd just

go out and kick it to pieces. That's

no way to act. Let 'em have their

fun, I say."

—Mr. Bashwater, **Freddy Goes To the North Pole**

"I always say, what's life without a

little spice of danger."

—Jinx the Cat, Freddy Goes To the North Pole

Responsibility

On a farm every bird and animal . . .

is supposed to do certain work. A

horse's duty is to draw ploughs and

wagons and buggies; and a dog's

duty is to bark at strangers

and do tricks and keep

an eye on the children and look

intelligent when his master talks

to him; and a cat's duty is to chase

mice, and purr when he's petted

and sleep in ladies' laps and sit on

the fence nights and sing. Some

animals don't have any special

duties. A pig's duty is just to be a

pig, which isn't very hard if you

have a good appetite.

—Freddy Goes To the North Pole

Freddy didn't sleep very well that night. The faces of all those trusting little animals who had brought their treasures into his bank for safekeeping crowded reproachfully into his dreams. For a poet to be president of the bank had always seemed to him something of a joke. For the first time he realized that it was a serious matter to be responsible for other people's property. But if he didn't catch the robbers, he'd make it good—down to the last kernel of corn.

—Freddy and the Ignormus

"Talk is easy; talk alone ain't worth

five cents a scuttleful.

What we want is

action."

—Jinx the Cat, **Freddy and
Simon the Dictator**

"But the ants aren't so much different from the folks in Centerboro that you've told me about. Lots of them work harder than they have to, just so they can have as shiny a car or as nice clothes as the people next door. Keeping up with the Joneses— isn't that what you call it?"

"That's right," said Freddy. "It's just showing off."

—Freddy and the Flying Saucer Plans

"Having a good time is all very

well, but I was brought up to think

that work was of some use in the

world too."

—Henrietta the Hen, **Freddy Goes To the North Pole**

When there's several things you can do, but they're all likely to turn out badly, and you can't decide— you're in a dilemma.

—Freddy the Pilot

Freddy was lying on his bed, reading.

He said he felt it was his duty to

read during his spare time, to improve

his mind. He was reading a book

on the lives of famous bandits. Of

course some books improve the

mind more than others.

—**Freddy and the Flying Saucer Plans**

Mr. Pomeroy was a robin, and the
head of the A.B.I.: the Animal
Bureau of Investigation. Freddy put
him to work at once on "what I
call," Freddy said, "the Case of the
Vanishing Martian." He always gave
a name like the title of a mystery
story to any case he wanted Mr.
Pomeroy to work on, because then
the robin felt that his work was

more important. And Freddy always

said that people do their best if

they think what they're doing is

important.

—Freddy and the Baseball Team from Mars

"Oh what a terrible thing is ambi-

tion!" he exclaimed. "Why could I

not have been content to remain in

obscurity, happy in the simple

quiet round of daily tasks, busy

with my books and my poetry? I

might in time have made quite a

name for myself as a poet."

—**Freddy and Mr. Camphor**

Like all lazy people, Freddy was capable of doing long stretches of really hard work. He was lazy in streaks . . . but he often spent more time and energy in getting out of a job than it would have taken to do the job in the first place.

—Freddy the Pied Piper

Like most lazy people, Freddy could work and work hard when he wanted to. But when he didn't want to—well, he just didn't want to.

—Freddy and Simon the Dictator

Freddy was a good executive: that is, he never liked to do any work he could get anyone else to do for him.

—Freddy the Politician

It was like

Mr. Bean

not to ask any

questions. He always

said that if his animals needed his

help, he was there to give it; other-

wise he thought it was better for

them to manage their own affairs.

—Freddy the Magician

Now of course Freddy could have run away, or he could have pretended that he was sick or something like that, but he was not that kind of a pig. If something unpleasant had to be done, he did it. He just wanted to be sure first that it really *had* to be done.

—Freddy and the Perilous Adventure

"I don't ever chase criminals on Sunday.... As a matter of fact, I don't see why a criminal shouldn't get Sunday off as much as anybody else."

—The Sheriff, **Freddy Plays Football**

Freddy knew that voice. It belonged to the sheriff. But Freddy did not turn round. For he knew that if there was a warrant out for his arrest . . . the sheriff would have to do his duty and arrest him, no matter how good friends they were.

—Freddy and the Perilous Adventure

Freddy always admitted frankly that he was lazy. And yet the more he had to do, the more he seemed to accomplish. He explained it this way: He said that when a lazy person once really gets started doing things, it's easier to keep on than it is to stop. He said it was as much of an effort to stop working and sit down as it was to get up and start working in the first place.

—Freddy the Pilot

Freddy always worked on the theory that it is better to do *some*thing, than just to sit and wait.

—Freddy Plays Football

Fortunately the wasps were home, hard at work chewing up wood to build a new house. But like all wasps and most people, they were glad of an excuse to knock off work for a little while.

—Freddy and Simon the Dictator

Animal Aspects

It always made Jinx mad to see anybody cry. He never cried himself, for he said it was a great waste of time. "If I feel bad about something," he said, "I go claw somebody. Then I feel better."

—**Freddy and the Ignormus**

"Cats—well, that's something else again. Being a  cat myself, it ill becomes me to praise their cleverness and resourcefulness, but you have asked me, and I shall not conceal the truth from you. The cat is the most accomplished animal ever created. If he wants to catch you—well, you're just caught, that's all."

—Jinx the Cat, **Freddy the Cowboy**

He shoved his jaw out determinedly,

and he tried to make his eyes as

piercing and hawklike as possible—

something that is not easy for a

pig, whose features are arranged on

a different plan. But he did come

close to something which was

a sort of combination of

George Washington and

Winston Churchill.

—Freddy and the Men from Mars

Charles, the rooster . . . was very economical and never wasted his best conversation on himself. Sometimes of course he said quite a good thing by mistake, but then he would save it up until someone came along and repeat it as if he had just thought of it.

—Freddy Goes To the North Pole

"It is the unalterable custom of all roosters to salute the dawn with appropriate musical notes."

—Charles the Rooster, **Freddy the Magician**

"When a new family moves into
the neighborhood, it's the polite
thing to go call on 'em. Us cats are
pretty particular about things like
that. Of course if a saucer of milk
is put out—well, it wouldn't be
good manners to just leave it
standing there."

—Jinx the Cat, **Freddy and the Spaceship**

Animal Aspects **75**

The only trouble with thinking was that he wouldn't think very hard for more than a few minutes without dropping off to sleep. This is not peculiar to pigs; many people have the same trouble."

—**Freddy Rides Again**

"You know thinking isn't my strong point, Freddy. I mean, I've got good brains, but they aren't the kind that think easily. They're the kind of brains that if you let 'em go their own way, they are as good as anybody's, but if you try to *make* them do anything, like a puzzle, they just won't work at all."

—Mrs. Wiggins, **Freddy the Detective**

Everything Freddy saw through
the small wavy window panes was
always so twisted out of shape that
he couldn't tell what it was. And
the dirt made it even harder. Freddy
liked it that way; he said that
things were twice as interesting
seen through those panes. It is not
especially exciting to see a cow
going by, but when you look out

and see a two-headed giant anteater,

it gives you something to wonder

about. That's the way Freddy felt

about it. Jinx, a frequent caller,

didn't agree. He said that the sight

of a lot of misshapen prehistoric

monsters prowling around outside

gave him cold chills. But cats don't

get as much fun out of imagining

things as other animals do.

—Freddy and the Spaceship

The next morning after breakfast [Freddy] went up to the cow barn to call on Mrs. Wiggins. She had been his partner for a while when he had been in the detective business, and he valued her advice highly. Like all poets, his schemes were apt to be brilliant, but sometimes highly impractical, and her sound common sense could always be trusted to pick out the weak spots in them. If more poets would seek the advice of cows, they would be less criticized for impractical behavior.

—Freddy and Mr. Camphor

Freddy very much wanted Jinx to go with him, but he knew that the surest way to get him was to pretend that he didn't. That's a cat all over. Let him think you don't want him to do some-thing, and he's crazy to do it.

—**Freddy and the Perilous Adventure**

Alligators are seldom very

experienced in affairs of the heart.

—**Freddy the Pilot**

"I don't know why it's so awful to call anybody pig-headed. Pigs— well, they're firm, they're determined, they don't just give up weakly when things go against them. If that's being pig-headed, then I'm glad I'm a pig."

—Freddy, **Freddy the Pied Piper**

I guess it didn't occur to Freddy that he was doing just what he had been lecturing the Pomeroys for doing: taking himself too seriously. Poets are inclined to do that. On the other hand, pigs, as a rule, seldom take themselves seriously enough. And it is perfectly true that if you don't take yourself seriously, nobody else will. It's hard to know just where to draw the line.

—Freddy and the Popinjay

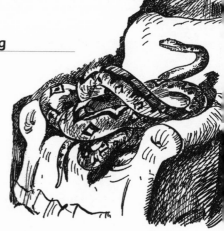

It is very hard to tell when a snake is sincere. Freddy could size up animals and people pretty well, but he admitted that snakes were beyond him. He said they always looked as if they were lying, even when they were telling the truth, because even in repose their faces always had a kind of sly smile.

—Freddy and the Dragon

"Camels are contrary. Nothing makes them happier than disappointing somebody."

—Freddy, **Freddy the Pied Piper**

Nobody ever bothers a beetle. A beetle's life is just one long picnic. Or should be. Then why do beetles hide under stones, and duck out of sight when they see a shadow? I'll tell you. They're born scared. Scared of things they can't see. Scared of things there aren't really any of. Like Ignormuses. If you could find one beetle that wasn't really scared of anything he couldn't see, that beetle would be a king.

—Freddy and the Ignormus

Freddy had talked to eagles before, so he was not surprised at this high-flown language. Eagles, since they are the national bird, have a great sense of their own dignity, and feel that just ordinary talk is beneath them.

—**Freddy and the Perilous Adventure**

Wasps are no diplomats. They don't

try to be tactful and persuasive

when they want something done;

they like to get out their stings

and get to work.

—Freddy and the Popinjay

Cows are not generally thought to make good detectives; they are too big and noisy to be much good at shadowing suspected persons, and they're not usually much interested in doing anything but just standing around and being cows. But Mrs. Wiggins's strong point was her common sense. . . . Many detectives, and other people who have problems to solve, could do well to follow

her example.

—Freddy and the Spaceship

"No sir," he said; "you don't get me up on any platform. Once you start that business you get like Charles—you just can't stop talking. Me, I'm a doer, not a talker." And when they asked him what it was he did, he said: "Sleep, mostly."

—Freddy and the Spaceship

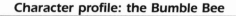

Bumble

bees make

excellent spies. They go blundering

along, bumping into things and

buzzing importantly, apparently

absorbed in their own rather stupid

business. Nobody pays much atten-

tion to them. But they have sharp

eyes and are good listeners. Nobody

fools a bumble bee, not for a minute.

—Freddy and the Men from Mars

Cats are persistent enough when

waiting for something to eat to

come out of a mouse hole, but they

won't keep up practicing singing,

or playing any instrument, unless

they get rewarded all the time.

—Freddy and the Men from Mars

All the animals on the neighboring

farms as well as at Mr. Bean's had

by this time heard about Freddy's

success as a detective, so the

meeting was a large one. A lot of

the woods animals, including Peter,

the bear, came. There were even a

few sheep, and if you know anything

about sheep, you will realize how

much interest the proposal for a jail

had created, for there is nothing

harder than to interest sheep in

matters of public policy.

—Freddy the Detective

Wasps are not cruel by nature; they just take pride in good workmanship. For a wasp, to sink his sting in a tender spot and make his victim yell, is the same as for a ballplayer to hit a homer. I don't suppose they ever think how it hurts.

—Freddy and Simon the Dictator

Mrs. Wiggins smiled, and if you have never seen a cow smile, you don't know how large and comfortable and pleasant a smile can be.

—Freddy's Cousin Weedly

Cows do a good deal of resting.
They are not very ambitious, and
few cows have ever made great
names for themselves in the world.
They would much rather sit around
in the shade and talk. But they are
often very wise animals, and their
opinions are well worth listening to.

—**Freddy's Cousin Weedly**

"You got any money in this bank, cat? I say, you got any money in here?"

"I've got *all* my money in here," said the cat. "That's the way I feel about how safe it is. And any other animal on this farm will tell you the same."

Freddy grinned, for he knew that Jinx had just eight cents in the bank. The cat had had a good deal more than that at various times. But cats never can seem to save any money, and Jinx was a free spender; when he got a little money it trickled right through his claws.

—Freddy and the Flying Saucer Plans

Moles in general have a name for being reliable and straightforward in their dealings, though often cranky and irritable.

—Freddy and the Flying Saucer Plans

House mice are taught all about

traps in the second grade, but field

mice get no such instruction;

indeed many field mice who live up

in the hills get no schooling at all.

—Freddy the Cowboy

The hardest animals to get up trips
for were cows. Cows aren't much
interested in what is going on in
the world. "It's hot and dusty out
on the road," they said, "and dogs
chase us, and automobiles make us
hurry in a very undignified way.
We'd rather stand round in the shade
and swish our tails and think."

—Freddy Goes to the North Pole

Cows are plain and there is nothing

they can do about it, but they are

very kindhearted animals, and it is

a pretty mean

man who will

deliberately

insult a cow.

**—Freddy the
Magician**

Cats very seldom make promises,

but when they do . . . their word

is as good as their bond.

—Freddy Goes to Florida

Even a cat cannot see anything in complete darkness, although all cats pretend that they can."

—**Freddy and Mr. Camphor**

Now, elephants aren't afraid of tigers but they are afraid of mice. If you ask an elephant why, he will giggle and say that the mouse might run up his trunk and tickle him and make him sneeze. Of course no mouse would have the nerve to do any such thing, but the elephants aren't taking any chances. Merely to think of it will make many elephants sneeze for half an hour.

—The Story of Freginald

"When somebody pulls a line on you that you don't like, you can't get anywhere by getting mad, or by arguing. Particularly when you can't fight. But we rabbits aren't fighters anyway, and there's one way we've learned to handle such things. Don't argue, don't oppose the fellow; agree with him. Take it right up and carry it on farther than he does. If he's sticky sweet to you, you be stickier and sweeter to him."

—Freddy and the Men from Mars

"People talk about scaredy-cats, but what they really ought to say is scaredy-mice. Mice are scareder than anybody."

"They are not!" said Quik, and Cousin Augustus said: "We're just smaller than other animals. We have to be careful."

—Freddy and the Flying Saucer Plans

Fleas are so nearly invisible that they find it easy to get away with things that wouldn't be tolerated for a moment in larger creatures. It is pretty hard to catch and punish a flea for bad manners.

—Freddy and Mr. Camphor

"Are you a man or are you a mouse?"

This is a question which always enrages mice, because it suggests that while men are bold and fearless, mice are the most timid and cowardly creatures on earth.... But many heroic deeds have been performed by mice. If more people knew about them they wouldn't be so scornful of these courageous little animals.

—**Freddy the Cowboy**

You have probably never seen a cow blush. And indeed the sight is unusual. There are two reasons for this. One is that cows are a very simple people, who do whatever they feel like doing and never realize that sometimes they ought to be embarrassed. . . . They are not sensitive. But they are kind and good natured, and if sometimes they seem rude, it is only due to their rather clumsy thoughtlessness.

The other reason is that cows' faces are not built for blushing.

—Freddy the Detective

Animal Aspects

Politics and the
Law of the Farm

"A country without a flag is as

silly . . . as a pig without a tail."

—Mrs. Wiggins, **Freddy the Politician**

"It's always safe to laugh and not

explain, if the other side seems to

be getting the best of an argument;

makes 'em think maybe they've said

something foolish and don't know it."

—Mrs. Wiggins, **Freddy the Politician**

"Nine out of ten political speeches are just a lot of hot air. Good gracious, even my own speeches bore me to death. I can hardly keep awake to finish them."

—Mr. Camphor, **Freddy and Simon the Dictator**

"Political speeches are not supposed to say anything important. The perfect political speech expresses a lot of noble but very vague sentiments in extremely high-flown language. That's what brings out the votes."

—Judge Anguish, **Freddy and Simon the Dictator**

[Freddy] solved the traffic problem
which had so snarled everything
up in most American cities. The
Frederick Bean Traffic Plan has now
been adopted in nearly every city
and town in the nation. The solution
was surprisingly simple: no parking
within the city limits at any time.
This made cars practically useless,
and people gave them up and took to
walking, thus improving the general
health, and cutting down the cost of
living. Indeed, its benefits have not
been exhausted yet.

—Freddy and Simon the Dictator

The pig was a very convincing speaker—not eloquent, but very matter-of-fact and practical, and therefore convincing.

—**Freddy and Simon the Dictator**

Charles, the rooster, stayed in the

office, because he was a very good

talker. . . . He was a good salesman.

That means that he could often

persuade animals to take trips that

they didn't really care about taking

at all.

—Freddy Goes To the North Pole

They liked Mr. Bashwater's speeches best, because he made a great many gestures and banged on the table and was so eloquent that he was always bathed in perspiration when he finally sat down.

—Freddy Goes To the North Pole

"Oh, dear, why did I think of Mr. Bean? What he'll say when he finds his gun missing I hate to think."

"You just said that he hardly ever says anything," put in Theodore.

"I guess that's what I'm afraid of. He won't talk; he probably won't even give me a licking."

"Well, then, I don't see what you're so scared of."

"It's what he'll think," said Freddy. "Whenever I see him around the barnyard, he'll look at me reproach-fully, and I'll know he's thinking: 'I'm disappointed in Freddy. I thought he was an honest pig.' You know, Theodore, that'll hurt more than all the lickings in the world."

—Freddy and the Ignormus

Of course Freddy could just have gone over to the cowbarn and said: "Simon's back. How about a meeting tonight?" But affairs of state are not conducted in such an off-hand manner. Mrs. Wiggins as a friend who had just knocked him into a barberry bush, and Mrs.

Wiggins as President of the F.A.R.

were two very different people. . . .

He had to put on a lot of dignity,

because if he didn't, none of the

others would either, and pretty

soon when Mrs. Wiggins gave an

official order, nobody would pay

any attention to it.

—Freddy and the Ignormus

The sheriff let the prisoners have parties, and go to movies and ball games because, he said, "I want to turn 'em into good citizens, and 'taint any training for good citizenship if you're locked up in a little cell all the time with no other citizens to talk to."

—**Freddy Plays Football**

"I do not see why solemnity is so desirable in this court. I do not see why good healthy laughter is incompatible with justice. Personally, sir, I feel that one good laugh is worth seventeen scholarly Supreme Court decisions."

"Why there, sir, you find me in complete accord."

—Uncle Solomon and Judge Willey,
Freddy and the Spaceship

"That's a fine way to treat me. Me, that's the best speaker this side of Albany! Me, who's responsible for what little patriotism there is on this farm."

"Rubbish!" said Freddy. "You'd have been responsible for putting 'em all to sleep if you'd gone on a little longer."

—**Freddy and Mr. Camphor**

The sheriff had found that the language of the law is pretty terrifying to guilty people, and so in cases like this he always used it. But there is one great trouble with the language of the law. The sentences are so long that very few people except judges can get through them without stopping to take a breath in the middle. And of course this spoils their impressiveness.

—Freddy and Mr. Camphor

"The trouble is," said Freddy,

"that all your fine words are just

decorations around big pieces of

nothing. One of your speeches is

like a beautiful frame without any

picture in it. It's like a beautiful

gold dish without any ice cream

in it. It's like—"

"I guess you're making a

speech yourself, aren't you?"

said Charles sourly.

"Yeah, I am at that," the pig

replied. "It

kind of creeps

up on you,

doesn't it?"

—Freddy and Mr. Camphor

Charles's speeches were so magnifi-

cent and noble sounding, he used

so many long and

high-flown words,

that very few ani-

mals could listen

to one of them

without becoming

wildly enthusiastic.

Just what they

were enthusiastic about they were

never quite certain, since, when

you thought about the speech afterwards, you were never sure what it meant. But the animals always enjoyed them, and they were indeed very useful, for when Charles sat down—or was pulled down, as sometimes happened—Freddy or Mrs. Wiggins would tell what action was proposed, and the enthusiasm was right there to carry it through. This is the real purpose of most speeches.

—Freddy and the Men from Mars

"It's just politics." He shivered. "It ain't much fun and it don't make sense, but you got to give folks what they expect."

—The Sheriff, **Freddy the Pied Piper**

Although he enjoyed nothing so

much as calling on a large audience

to rise and overthrow something

or other, he seldom got around to

demanding action—first, because

he liked hearing his own voice, and

second—well, there isn't any second.

—Freddy Plays Football

"Of course," the sheriff went on, "there may be some law I don't know about. Lots of times there's little unimportant laws get passed, and my goodness, you can't even find 'em in the index. And you go along, thinking you're minding your own business, and then bang! you trip over one of 'em, and you're in a peck of trouble."

—Freddy and the Men from Mars

Experience had taught Mr. Metacarpus
the quickest way to settle [a dispute]
was to get the person that made
the most noise and the one that
said the least together in his office
and thrash the question out.

—Freddy the Magician

"I suppose the President will want to

see them, and all the senators will

want to ask them questions and

find out if they are Republicans

or Democrats."

—**Freddy and the Men from Mars**

This would have stumped almost
anyone but Mrs. Wiggins. But she
had been to Washington and seen
how Congress worked, and she
knew that if you can't get action
from a big meeting, the thing to do
is make the meeting smaller. And
the way to do that is to appoint
a committee.

—**Freddy and the Popinjay**

The rooster was a fine speaker and he used words so beautifully that they all liked to hear him, although they didn't always know what he was talking about. Neither did he, sometimes, but nobody cared, for, as with all good speakers, what he

said wasn't half as important as the noble way he said it.

—**Freddy the Detective**

When Freddy made a speech he said what he had to say and sat down. But when Charles made one, he said everything he had to say in six different ways, each more high-sounding, and with bigger words, than the last one.

—Freddy and the Perilous Adventure

• • •

Imagination

If you are going to write poetry,

you need two things. You need

quiet and you need coolness. You

can't have a lot of people talking to

you, and you can't be all hot and

sticky. Of course you also need

paper and pencil. So Freddy always

took these along, and he would lie

on the bank and write a little, and

then think a long time, and then

write a little more. Sometimes he

would do so much thinking and so

little writing that Theodore thought

he was asleep. But Freddy said no,

he was just thinking very hard.

—**Freddy and the Ignormus**

Usually when Freddy started a poem, he began with an idea, something he wanted to say. Then he took the idea and fitted verses to it. It was a good deal like eating bread and jam and trying to make them come out even. . . . It was very easy for Freddy to write verses, but not so easy to get good ideas. It was as if he had lots and lots of bread, but not very much jam. That is the trouble with a good many poets. They make very nice verses, but you can hardly taste the jam in them at all.

—Freddy and the Popinjay

"That's what always happens when I

begin to think about my poems.

Pretty soon I begin to wonder if I

haven't said just the opposite of

what I mean."

—Freddy, **Freddy and the Popinjay**

Madame Delphine used very beautiful

and high-flown language when she

was telling fortunes, but when she

sat and rocked she used just ordinary

language like anybody else. And

Louise noticed that when she used

ordinary language she said much

more interesting things. He tried it

with his poems, and he found that

the simpler they were, the better

people liked them. He was rather

smart to notice this, for lots of

really important people never find

it out at all.

—The Story of Freginald

Like all poets, [Freddy's] schemes were apt to be brilliant, but sometimes highly impractical, and [Mrs. Wiggins'] sound common sense could always be trusted to pick out the weak spots in them. If more poets would seek the advice of cows, they would be less criticized.

—Freddy and Mr. Camphor

"Thinking's like fishing. You bait your hook and throw it in the water, but if there aren't any fish around, you naturally can't catch anything."

—Mr. Camphor, **Freddy and Simon the Dictator**

"Enter the poet's lair. See the poet himself at work, hammering out the hexameters, enshrining in deathless verse his own two-cent

exploits, his eye in fine frenzy rolling—nay, practically popping out of his head in self-admiration—"

—Freddy and Simon the Dictator

Mr. Webb was the engineer and Mrs. Webb was the passenger. "All aboard," Mr. Webb would say: "All aboard for Persia, Mesopotamia, China and points east." Then, after a minute he would say: "Here we are, mother. Just pulling into the station at Samarkand." . . . They had lots of fun that way, and Mrs. Webb always said it was much the best way to travel. There was no bother of tickets, or catching trains, and you always slept in your own bed at night. And when you got tired of traveling, you just stopped, and there you were at home.

—**Freddy's Cousin Weedly**

Your true poet will make his verses, no matter how painful his life may be. In prison, or tied to the stake with the savages dancing about him in a yelling circle—still he will sing. At least that is what Freddy said. He admitted privately, however, that he couldn't compose poetry when he had a stomach-ache.

—Freddy and the Men from Mars

The animals thought and thought....
All this thinking going on depressed
Mr. Boomschmidt even more. "My
goodness," he said," . . . I wish you'd
stop it. You don't catch me thinking,
do you? I guess not! I've got enough
trouble without doing that."

The animals said: "Yes, sir," and
went right on thinking—all except
Oscar, who said that it made him
have bad dreams.

—The Story of Freginald

Now Freddy had a good deal of imagination, and people like that are apt to think up so many ways of doing a thing that they can't decide among them, and then they don't do anything.

—Freddy and the Perilous Adventure

But that is often the time, just on the edge of sleep, when people do think of the best things. The trouble is that they are seldom strong-minded enough to jump up and put their ideas into action at once. And so they drop off to sleep and the ideas are lost.

—**Freddy and the Perilous Adventure**

Nobody likes to have a poem he

has just made pulled to pieces.

—Freddy Plays Football

If Freddy hadn't fallen asleep when
he got this far, the poem would
have been a great deal longer. In
fact, it might well have gone on
forever, for Freddy was like a good
many other poets—he never could
seem to find a good stopping place.
Even when he had nothing more to
say, it seemed always as if the last
stanza he had written didn't really
make the right kind of ending, so
he would start another. But, of
course, sooner or later, he would
fall asleep, and as it was usually
"sooner" in Freddy's case, none of
his poems are very long ones.

—Freddy and the Popinjay

"I'm all hot from sleeping so hard. I wonder why it is that it makes you just as hot to sleep hard as to work hard? I suppose it's because even in my sleep my mind is so active."

—Freddy, **Freddy and the Popinjay**

"I don't like sad poetry.... Dear me,

there are enough cheerful things in

the world without thinking up such

mournful ones to write poems about."

—Emma the Duck, **Freddy and the Popinjay**

"I've said before and I'll say it
again . . . that all these ideas
aren't healthy. Sulphur and
molasses—that's what he needs.
There isn't an idea that a good
dose of sulphur and molasses
won't cure."

—Mrs. Wiggins, **Freddy and the Popinjay**

"How true it is that the great artist

never gets anything but ridicule

from his own friends."

—J. J. Pomeroy the Robin, **Freddy and the Popinjay**

Honesty

"An honest opinion is worth more

than all the flattery in the world."

—Freddy, **Freddy Goes Camping**

"I guess people always look ridiculous when they try to look like something they aren't," said Mr. Camphor. "Whether it's false whiskers they put on, or just a very noble and heroic expression."

—**Freddy and Simon the Dictator**

"I'm going back to talk to old Whibley. He's got ideas, if only you can get 'em out of him."

"Not me," said Jinx. "I've had enough of his sarcastic cracks."

"He tells you the truth about your-self," said Freddy. "Maybe it'd be a good idea to hear it once in a while."

"Not me, either," said Jacob. "My father used to tell me the truth about myself once in a while, and it was usually accompanied with a licking."

—**Freddy the Politician**

"I wouldn't trust him much. He's using lies every day, and if he got mad at you, he'd pick up the handiest thing to get even with. And what has he always got handy?— a good, fat lie."

—Mrs. Wiggins,
Freddy Plays Football

"Keep your word, no matter what it costs you—that's my motto."

—Mr. Doty, **Freddy Plays Football**

"Do you *like* being honest?" he asked.

"Not exactly," said Freddy truthfully.

"Then why do you do it when you don't have to?"

"I don't know. I suppose maybe because Mr. Bean thinks I'm honest. I sort of want him to be right.

"H'm," said Mr. Golcher. "Nobody ever thought *I* was honest, I guess. . . I suppose I might try it some time."

—**Freddy and the Perilous Adventure**

"You can't ever make the chief believe that anybody would cheat him. He wants to think everybody is as honest as he is."

It embarrassed Mr. Boomschmidt to be praised, and he blushed deeply. "I'm not honest at all," he said. "I mean, I'm not any honester than you are, Leo, and I'll thank you not to accuse me of it."

—Freddy the Pilot

Old Whibley opened his eyes wide and nodded approvingly. "Clever speech," he said.

"Clever nothing," said Mrs. Wiggins. "It's the truth."

"That's why it's clever," said the owl.

—Freddy the Politician

"Look,
Sniffy,
Robin Hood
was made an outlaw unjustly, by
people in power who were wicked.
But Mr. Bean isn't wicked, and if he
outlawed you for fighting rabbits, it
wouldn't be unjust. Robin Hood
knew he was right, but you'd know
you were wrong."

—Freddy the Pilot

Honesty **173**

"While, of course, the winner should

have a prize, there is every reason

why the losers should have prizes

too. For after all, the winner has

won; the knowledge

that he is the

best should be

enough of a

prize for him.

Whereas the loser, ladies and gentle-
men, gets nothing. Not only is he
disappointed because he has lost,
but he gets nothing to make up to
him for the time and trouble it has
cost him. Indeed, in the future...
the prizes will be awarded *only* to
the losers. That seems to us a much
fairer arrangement."

—Jinx the Cat, **Freddy and the Popinjay**

"Some statements mean just the
opposite of what they say. Suppose
I say that I never tell the truth.
Well, if that is true, then I always
lie. But if I always lie, then I'm
lying when I say I never tell the
truth. So my statement really
means that I am truthful."

—Freddy, **Freddy Goes Camping**

"Tell a big lie, and the first time, nobody believes it much. Like the Beans having rabbit stew. But keep repeating it, and by and by somebody says: 'I wonder if maybe they *did* have rabbit stew!' And then it's

told and repeated so often that everybody comes to believe it."

—Freddy,
**Freddy and Simon
the Dictator**

No dog in the history of the world

has ever been known to tell a lie,

and that is why man

has selected the dog as

his chief friend among

the animals.

—Freddy Goes to the North Pole

Deer lead very secluded lives, and although they are curious, they are too timid ever to venture into the more cultivated regions where important things are going on. A quite small bit of gossip will last a deer for a month, and he'll tell it over and over to all his friends, and they hurry to tell it to their friends, until it is known all over the north country. But they are very honest animals and never gossip maliciously.

—Freddy Goes to the North Pole

As for "the latest Paris creations,"
Freddy knew perfectly well that
Miss Peebles made every hat she
sold right in her own shop. But as
everybody else in Centerboro knew
it too, it couldn't be said that Miss
Peebles was trying to deceive anybody. "I guess it's just advertising,"
Freddy thought. "If it sounds nice,
nobody expects it to mean anything."

—Freddy and the Popinjay

The more honest you are in an
argument, the better chance you
have of winning.

—Freddy and the Popinjay

Horse Sense

"It is my experience that nothing

that is worth getting is easy to get."

—Charles the Rooster, **Freddy Goes to Florida**

"It's better to be too tender-hearted,

I always say, than to run the risk

of getting too hard."

—Mrs. Wiggins,
Freddy the Detective

"If you like something, or want

something, or are afraid of some-

thing yourself, you're pretty apt

to think that everybody else in

the world likes or wants or is

afraid of the same thing."

—Mrs. Bean, **Freddy Goes Camping**

Jinx . . . grinned at the pig, but after that he didn't say any more about it. He was smart enough to know that you don't gain anything by crowing over your victories.

—Freddy Goes Camping

"When every-thing seems like a hopeless mess, the thing to do is stir it up good. Then something always comes to the top that you can use."

—Freddy, **Freddy and the Men from Mars**

"The way to make life more interesting isn't to sit around and growl about it. It is to go out and hunt up something."

—Mrs. Wiggins, **Freddy the Cowbo**

And then they knew that Spring had come and it was time for them to be starting back home. "Well I for one shall be glad to get back," said Mrs. Wiggins. "We've had a grand time traveling, but home's a pretty good place to be."

—Freddy Goes to Florida

"You know, if we knew everything beforehand, things wouldn't be much fun, would they?"

That was really one of the smartest things Freddy ever said.

—**Freddy the Pied Piper**

"My land, all the great inventions

were discovered by curious people.

What's curiosity anyway but trying

to find out something you don't

know."

—Mrs. Wiggins, **Freddy Rides Again**

When Mr. Bean didn't know the

answer to a question he kept still.

He kept still now. Some people

would have said they thought maybe

it was this, or maybe it was that,

but not Mr. Bean. For he knew

what lots of people never learn:

that no answer is better than the

wrong one, and sometimes than

the right one too.

—Freddy and the Perilous Adventure

"It doesn't cost much to pass out a

few words of praise.

And it sure gets

results."

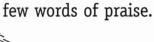

—Freddy,
Freddy Goes Camping

"There's always two sides to every question. . . . And the funny part of it is, both sides are usually right. There wouldn't ever be any arguments if one side was always right and the other always wrong."

—J. J. Pomeroy the Robin, **Freddy and the Popinjay**

In his experience as a detective,

Freddy had found that those who

are always protesting that they

have nothing to hide were usually

concealing some pretty awful stuff.

—Freddy and the Men from Mars

"It's always a waste of time explaining to people that you're not as big a fool as they think you are."

—Whibley the Owl, *Freddy and the Bean Home News*

"No joke is good if it hurts somebody's feelings."

—Cy the Pony,
Freddy Rides Again

"There's two ends to a joke, and it depends on which end you get hold of whether it's fun or not."

—Cousin Weedly,
Freddy's Cousin Weedly

As a general thing, if anybody expects an apology, the polite thing is to give it to them. It saves a lot of wear and tear.

—Freddy and the Perilous Adventure

"That's the trouble with detective

work. . . . Too many clues

are worse than

none at all."

—Freddy,
Freddy Plays Football

"Watching mirrors all the time

just makes us look anxious and

a little foolish."

—Freddy, **Freddy the Magician**

You can admire yourself in a mirror for quite a long time, but after a while it stops being fun. At first you're pretty pleased, and you look at yourself full-face and smile and try different expressions, and then you try to see if your profile isn't pretty noble—but then you begin to notice things that aren't so good.

—Freddy Rides Again

"Any hen can crow if she wants to, better than any rooster that ever was hatched."

—Henrietta the Hen, **Freddy Goes to Florida**

"Agree with him, pig. You can make

him do anything by always taking

his side of the argument away

from him."

—Mr. Webb, **Freddy and Mr. Camphor**

"Talk causes too much trouble. Look at the wars and things these humans have got into, and all on account of talk. The minute that animals begin to talk a lot they'll be having wars too. Rabbits will declare war on chipmunks, and gangs of cows will ambush horses. . . ."

—Cy the Pony, **Freddy the Cowboy**

"The trouble with believing that

certain things bring bad luck . . .

is not that they really do bring it,

but that you believe they do. In

believing it, you sort of prepare

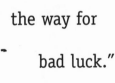

the way for

bad luck."

—Mrs. Church,
Freddy the Pied Piper

"If you lose your temper in a fight, you're licked before you start."

—Mr. Bean, Freddy the Pilot

In a fight, or in a contest of any kind, the one who keeps his temper has an advantage that is equal to two shotguns and a small cannon.

—Freddy the Magician

"We heard it all," said Mrs. Wiggins.
"Robert, what's a yokel?"

"Search me," said Robert. "But I don't
think he meant it as a compliment."

"No," said the cow. But he's afraid
of me or he wouldn't be calling me
names. That's what people always
do when they're scared."

—Freddy the Politician

"I remember what my Uncle Ajax

used to say. 'Children,' he said, 'are

not strictly speaking animals at all.

They're not grown-ups, either. More

like some kind of very active bug.

A bug with a habit of making loud

noises that don't mean anything.

But you can get along with them

if you can forget how funny they

look, and if you remember to treat

them as if they had a lot of sense.

That, of course,' Uncle Ajax said, 'is

important in dealing with grown-

ups too. In fact,' he said, 'although

in theory kids and grown-ups are

different species, in practice there

ain't enough difference between

'em to fill the hole in a doughnut.'"

—Leo the Lion,
Freddy and the Baseball Team from Mars

• • •

People, Pigs, and
Popular Opinion

"Handsome is as handsome does,"

Freddy would say. "And if it's a

choice between being handsome

and a second helping of chocolate

layer cake, I'll take the cake

every time."

—Freddy, **Freddy Goes To the North Pole**

Pigs understand boys pretty well, perhaps because they are so much alike. If fathers and mothers who have trouble with bad boys would consult pigs oftener, they would profit by it. But perhaps that is too much to ask.

—Freddy and Mr. Camphor

"Men that keep old bookstores are supposed to have long white beards and be covered with dust, just as college professors are supposed to be so absent-minded that they ought to be locked up, and army sergeants are supposed to be rough, tough men with jaws like flatirons. As a matter of fact most of these people aren't like that at all.... Just the opposite, in fact."

—Mr. Tweedle, **Freddy the Pilot**

He was kind of old fashioned about having animals talk; it made him uneasy, and he always said animals should be seen not heard. So Freddy and his friends seldom said anything to him; if there was anything important they told Mrs. Bean. He never asked her where such information came from. But of course he knew, and was pretty proud, secretly, of having such clever animals.

—Freddy Goes Camping

J.J. was a robin, and he was singing the only song a robin can sing, which all of the guests had heard thousands of times. But because he was all dressed up in a lot of elegant and fancy feathers, they expected to hear an elegant and fancy song; and because they expected to hear it, they did hear it. It was certainly true, Freddy thought, that fine feathers make fine birds.

—Freddy and the Popinjay

Pigs don't have as sensitive skins

as people do, but their feelings are

just as easily hurt.

—Freddy the Pilot

All anybody could see was the barnyard with the buildings grouped round it. I guess no stranger would have thought it specially beautiful or picturesque. But of course it was their own home, and that made a difference.

—Freddy the Cowboy

"It's not the unmanageable animals

that give us trouble, it's the

unmanageable people."

—Mr. Boomschmidt, **Freddy the Pilot**

"Umph" is a word that pigs use only
when they are thoroughly disgusted
with people. If a pig calls you an
umph, you have a right to get mad
about it—unless, of course, you
happen to be one.

—Freddy Goes To the North Pole

"A pig—*as* pig—can be a very handsome animal. I should be the last to deny it. On the other hand, a pig looks like a pig and a man looks like a man. No pig wants to look like a man and—per contra, conversely, and vice versa—no man wants to be told that he looks like a pig."

—Mr. Boomschmidt, **Freddy and the Perilous Adventure**

"When I was a girl, animals behaved

the way you expected them to. Cats

and mice didn't go out walking

together and pigs didn't read

newspapers."

—Mrs. Bean, **Freddy Goes To the North Pole**

His staff was one which J. Edgar
Hoover himself might have envied.
For clever as an F.B.I. man may be,
he cannot hide under a pie-plant
leaf like a rabbit; he cannot sit
under a window sill and listen
to a conversation without being
noticed, like a bumblebee.

—Freddy and the Baseball Team from Mars

But the trousers bothered his legs,

and he stumbled over roots and

tripped over vines and fell into

holes until, long before he reached

the creek, he was so bruised and

hot and out of breath that he sat

down on a log to rest. "My good-

ness," he said to himself, "I'm glad

I'm not a man! How they ever manage to do anything or get anywhere in all these clumsy hot clothes I can't imagine! Lords of creation, they call themselves! Humph, I'd rather be a pig anytime."

—Freddy the Detective

Of course there are some artists who say that they don't care whether other people praise their work or not; if they themselves are pleased with it, that is enough. I am glad to say that Freddy wasn't that kind. He liked being praised just as much as you and I do.

—Freddy and Mr. Camphor

"I suppose they've got a right to search my place," said Freddy, "but I don't see why they have to criticize my housekeeping."

Jinx grinned. "I don't either," he said. "People hadn't ought to criticize you for something you don't do."

—Freddy Plays Football

Humor

When everybody's laughing it

is pretty hard to keep

a sober face.

—**Freddy and
the Popinjay**

Mrs. Wiggins only said that a joke

was a joke, and old ones, that had

stood the test of time, were the best.

—Freddy the Pilot

"Hi, old pig!" said the cat, slapping him on the back. "Golly, we've been worried! We thought the old sausage grinder had got you at last." Freddy winced. It is not very tactful to mention sausage or bacon to a pig.

—Freddy and Mr. Camphor

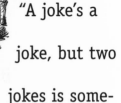

I wouldn't want to bring in an animal that was brighter than the prisoners are; they might think I was trying to teach 'em something, and prisoners and school kids are a lot alike: there ain't anything that makes 'em madder than to think you're trying to teach 'em something."

—The Sheriff, **Freddy the Pied Piper**

"A joke's a joke, but two jokes is something else again."

—The Sheriff, **Freddy and the Popinjay**

"Curiosity killed the cat. I wonder

how many million times I've heard

that! As if cats were any more

curious than other animals. I bet

if all the goats curiosity has killed

were laid end to end they'd

reach from here to

San Francisco."

—Jinx the Cat,
Freddy Rides Again

"There ain't anybody can be a clown
and stay happy. . . . Because there
ain't anybody can tell the same
jokes over twice a day, week after
week, year after year, and not get
pretty sour. When you tell a joke
once, it's funny. But when you tell
it the two hundred and seventh
time, it makes you cry. . . . Why,
what do you suppose is the reason
for clowns painting their faces and
wearin' false noses? . . . It's so's the
audience can't see how mournful
they look."

—Bill the Clown, **The Story of Freginald**

"I expect [Freddy's] got another idea," said the cow placidly.

"I dunno where he gets 'em all," said Hank. "In fact, I dunno as I know what an idea is. I never had any myself, I'm thankful to say. They look kind of unpleasant to me— make you run around and yell. Folks are better without them."

—Hank and Mrs. Wiggins, The Clockwork Twin

"The politer you are at a party,

the more you can eat without

anybody noticing it."

—Mrs. Wiggins, **Freddy's Cousin Weedly**

"My Uncle Ajax was a tough old fighter. But he said to me, he said: 'There's only two things, Leo, a lion ought to run from: one is spring housecleaning, and the other is goblins.'"

—Leo the Lion,
Freddy and the Men from Mars

"My Uncle Ajax always said: Never explain a weak joke. Just change the subject quick."

—Leo the Lion
Freddy and the Baseball Team from Mars

Mrs. Peppercorn said: "Someone raided Mrs. Lafayette Bingle's icebox the other night. A ham was taken."

Freddy frowned. "No matter how low he had sunk, no pig would take a ham," he said.

—Freddy and the Dragon

"A cat has nine lives," said Freddy with a grin.

"Oh yeah?" said Jinx. "And suppose it was wrong. Where'd I be?"

"You'd be famous," said Georgie. "You'd be a martyr to science. The cat that sacrificed himself to find out the truth."

"There's more than one way to skin a cat," said the dog with a snicker.

"I don't know why all these proverbs are so down on cats," Jinx said.

—Freddy and Mr. Camphor

I don't know if you have ever

been kissed by a cow, but it is

a large-scale operation.

—Freddy the Cowboy

"We used to play a game," Freddy
said; "sit around and make faces,
and the most horrible one got
the prize."

"You must show me your prizes
some time," Mr. Camphor said.
"I'll bet you've got a roomful."

—Freddy Goes Camping

A pig's face is built for smiling, and
Freddy never looked so handsome
as when he was squealing with
laughter.

—Freddy Goes To the North Pole

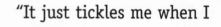

"It just tickles me when I think I'm floating around all cool and pretty like a lump of ice cream in an ice cream soda, and then plunk!—my back hits bottom. It's me, thinking I'm one thing, and really being something else; that's what makes it funny. . . ."

—Freddy and the Popinjay

Snakes don't usually care much about books, probably because they haven't any hands to hold them with.

—Freddy the Pilot

Now Mr. Camphor stopped giggling. "Maybe you're right Bannister," he said, "but it isn't so that giggle and the world giggles with you. The world just thinks you're silly."

—**Freddy and Simon the Dictator**

"I know what I look like, and it's

no special pleasure to keep being

reminded of it."

—Freddy the Cowboy

"I'm not specially interested in sawing

anybody in two. I wouldn't care to

try it on anybody I

liked, and on any-

body I didn't like it

would be sort of a

waste of time, since

apparently they

don't stay sawed."

—Freddy, **Freddy the Magician**

"I don't ever listen to what I say myself. I don't suppose I even hear it. That's perfectly natural, isn't it? . . . After all, what I want is to hear what the other fellow says."

—Mr. Boomschmidt, **Freddy the Magician**

"Personally I think all their talk about being so wise is a lot of whoosh. It takes more than a pair of big eyes and a bad disposition to set up in the wisdom business."

—Freddy the Magician

Spiders are not generally great
travelers. Of course they have
plenty of legs, but their legs
are too short.

—**Freddy Plays Football**

It is no joke ordering dinner when

you have an elephant as a guest.

—Freddy the Pilot

"If you want to get race records broken, instead of firing a pistol at the starting line, you ought to ring a dinner bell at the finish."

—Freddy, **Freddy Plays Football**